Dirty Bertie

TROUBLE!

DAVID ROBERTS WRITTEN BY **ALAN MACDONALD**

Stripes

Dirty Bertie
Collect all the
Dirty Bertie books!

Dirty Bertie

TROUBLE!

For Felix and Josh ~ D R
For Niav, who has all the Bertie books
~ A M

STRIPES PUBLISHING LTD
An imprint of the Little Tiger Group
1 Coda Studios, 189 Munster Road,
London SW6 6AW

www.littletiger.co.uk

A paperback original
First published in Great Britain in 2020

Characters created by David Roberts
Text copyright © Alan MacDonald, 2020
Illustrations copyright © David Roberts, 2020

ISBN: 978-1-78895-025-1

MIX
Paper from
responsible sources
FSC® C020471

The Forest Stewardship Council® (FSC®) is a global, not-for-profit organization dedicated to the
promotion of responsible forest management worldwide. FSC® defines standards based on agreed
principles for responsible forest stewardship that are supported by environmental, social, and
economic stakeholders. To learn more, visit www.fsc.org

10 9 8 7 6 5 4 3 2 1

Contents

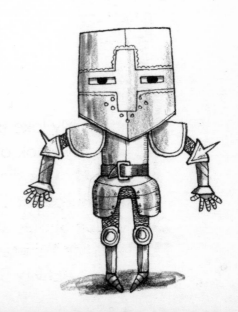

TROUBLE!

CHAPTER 1

It was another Monday morning. Bertie and his friends were walking to school.

"So what did you do yesterday?" asked Bertie.

"Mostly homework," sighed Eugene. "We've got that maths test, remember?"

Bertie stopped in his tracks.

"Maths test?" he said. "When?"

Dirty Bertie

"Today!" said Eugene. "Miss Boot's testing us on our homework."

"Don't tell me you've forgotten?" said Darren.

Bertie nodded – of course he'd forgotten. He'd meant to do the homework but there'd been so many other things to do, like watch TV.

"Trust you, Bertie!" grinned Darren. "How are you going to pass the test?"

Bertie shrugged. "I'll just have to guess like last time."

He hated maths tests. Why couldn't Miss Boot test him on something he knew – like the world record for burping?

"Maybe she'll have forgotten," he suggested.

"Huh! Not Miss Boot," said Eugene.

Dirty Bertie

"Well, maybe she'll be away then," said Bertie. "Mr Weakly's always off sick."

But when they arrived Miss Boot was there as usual. Bertie couldn't remember her ever missing a day of school. Germs were probably too scared to go near her.

Dirty Bertie

"Well, I hope you all remembered your homework," she said. "I promised you a maths test so we can all look forward to it after break."

Bertie slumped back in his chair. He was doomed. Everyone apart from him seemed to have done their homework. Know-All Nick had probably spent the whole weekend revising. Bertie knew his mum would go mad if she found out he'd watched TV instead of doing his schoolwork. There had to be some way he could get out of the test!

Just then he caught sight of Miss Boot's coffee flask poking out of her bag. It gave him a brilliant idea. What if he could make a magic potion? It always worked in stories, especially if you went to Hogwarts. Magic potions could do

Dirty Bertie

all sorts of things, such as making a test disappear! And luckily he was brilliant at magic. His gran had given him a magic set and he'd already learned to make a plastic ball vanish from a cup. All he had to do was make the maths test vanish from Miss Boot's mind! How hard could it be?

Dirty Bertie

The tricky part was getting Miss Boot to drink the magic potion, but that was where the flask came in. If he could somehow sneak the potion into her flask, she'd drink it just like coffee. Bertie sat back – the plan *had* to work. It was his only chance.

CHAPTER 2

The bell went for break and everyone filed out. This was Bertie's chance. Miss Boot was busy preparing the test papers. Her bag hung from her chair, unguarded. As Bertie walked past, he grabbed the flask and stuffed it under his jumper.

Outside he showed Darren and Eugene his prize.

Eugene stared boggle-eyed. "Where did you get that?"

"From Miss Boot's bag," replied Bertie. "It's her coffee flask."

"I know what it is!" said Eugene. "But what are *you* doing with it?"

"Put it away!" warned Darren. "Here comes Know-All Nick."

Bertie stuffed the flask back under his jumper. Nick stopped to stare at him suspiciously.

"What have you got there?" he demanded.

"Nothing," said Bertie. "And it's none of your business, anyway."

"Really?" said Nick. "If you say so."

They waited for him to leave, then Bertie explained his master plan.

"A magic potion? You think that'll work?" grinned Darren.

"Why not? I'm great at magic," said Bertie.

"You're mad," said Eugene. "If Miss Boot finds out you've taken her flask she'll go potty."

"She won't. I'll put it back after break," said Bertie. "She won't suspect a thing."

"She will when she drinks her coffee!" laughed Darren.

"But then the potion will work," said Bertie. "And the test will vanish from her head like magic!"

Eugene shook his head. "I still say you're crazy. You risk it if you want, but count me out. My mum says you always get me into trouble."

He walked off.

Bertie stared for a moment then turned to Darren. "What about you?"

"I'm in!" Darren smiled. "I'll do anything to avoid a maths test!"

Bertie wasn't exactly sure what ingredients they needed for a magic potion. Obviously bats' wings or dragons' claws would be ideal but they weren't easy to find in the playground. Instead he collected a handful of nettles and dandelions while Darren found a spider's web. Bertie squished them all into Miss Boot's flask. He added water from the drinking fountain and gave it a good shake. They stared at the gloopy liquid.

"YUCK! It looks disgusting!" said
Darren. "She'll never drink that."

"Maybe not," agreed Bertie. "We
need to make it look more like coffee."

He found a puddle and scooped up
a handful of mud. In it went turning the
potion a murky brown.

"That's better. Now what?" asked
Darren.

"Now we make a spell to add the

17

magic," replied Bertie.

He thought for a moment before shutting his eyes. He circled his hands over the potion, chanting in a low voice:

"Hocus-pocus, pants and vest,
Make Miss Boot forget this test."

"That should do it," said Bertie.

"Great, but what if she doesn't drink it?" frowned Darren.

"She will," said Bertie. "She always has a coffee in the morning."

"First we'll have to get her flask back," Darren pointed out.

"True," said Bertie. "You keep her talking while I sneak it into her bag."

When the bell went, they filed into school and waited for Miss Boot outside the classroom. Soon she came marching down the corridor. Bertie stared. Oh no, she was carrying her bag – she must have taken it with her to the staffroom! How could he put the flask back now? But it was too late to change the plan because Darren had stepped out to stop her.

"Oh, miss, I think Nick's stuck up a tree," he said.

"A tree? What are you talking about?" snapped Miss Boot.

Bertie didn't wait to hear Darren's unlikely explanation. He slipped into the classroom and looked around. Where could he leave the flask so Miss Boot would find it? In a panic he left it on her chair and hurried to his seat.

Seconds later, Miss Boot walked in.

"Hurry up and sit down," she said, thumping her bag down on her desk.

Bertie gave Darren a nod as he took his seat beside him.

Miss Boot glared. "Before we start, has anyone seen my coffee flask?" she demanded. "It was in my bag this morning but now seems to have disappeared."

Dirty Bertie

The class shook their heads. Miss
Boot scowled. Someone had to know
something, she was sure of it. She pulled
out her chair and did a double take. The
flask was right there on her seat. She
certainly hadn't left it there, because she
always took her coffee to the staffroom.
She narrowed her eyes.
*Someone is playing
tricks,* she thought.
*And whoever is responsible,
I will find out.*

CHAPTER 3

Miss Boot was busy explaining the maths test to the class.

"Well?" whispered Eugene. "Did you do it?"

Bertie pointed to the flask.

"Seriously? You've put a magic potion in there?" asked Eugene.

"You missed all the fun," said Bertie.

Dirty Bertie

"And the best part is it looks exactly like coffee!"

"You're bonkers," said Eugene. "What did you put in it?"

Bertie shrugged. "Just the usual potion stuff – nettles, cobwebs, a bit of mud…"

"MUD?" squeaked Eugene. "What if she drinks it?"

"She's meant to drink it," said Bertie. "Otherwise it won't work."

Eugene shook his head. Bertie had done some crazy things in his time but this beat them all.

"She'll probably be sick!" he said.

"She won't," snorted Bertie.

"She will if it's full of mud and cobwebs!" said Eugene. "What if you make her ill?"

Bertie looked a little worried.

Dirty Bertie

"It's only a magic potion," he said.

"Yes, but how do you know what it'll do?" said Eugene. "Her hair might fall out or her tongue could turn blue. Anything could happen! What if she grows horns or something?"

Bertie hadn't thought of this. In stories magic sometimes had unexpected results. He only wanted Miss Boot to forget the maths test, not to sprout horns! Surely a little mud and cobwebs couldn't do any real harm?

Dirty Bertie

On the other hand they'd added
weeds, nettles and who knew what.
What if the potion did make her ill? He
stared at the flask sitting on Miss Boot's
desk. He was starting to think this
wasn't such a great idea after all.

Just then Miss Boot finished what
she was saying and picked up her flask.
Bertie watched in horror as she started
to unscrew the lid! He had to stop her
before it was too late!

CHAPTER 4

Bertie's hand shot up.

"Yes!" groaned Miss Boot. "What is it, Bertie?"

"Can we open a window?" asked Bertie, playing for time.

"A window? What for?" said Miss Boot.

"I'm too hot," moaned Bertie. "I'm

26

burning up!"

Miss Boot rolled her eyes.

"Is anyone else too hot?" she asked.

No one was. Nevertheless she set down her flask and went to open a window. Anything so they could get on with the test in peace.

Back at her desk she picked up the pile of papers.

"Right, let's get started," she said. "Nicholas, hand round these test papers, please."

Bertie breathed out. Miss Boot seemed to have forgotten her coffee – at least for the moment.

He tried to stay calm. Facing the maths test was bad enough, but now he couldn't take his eyes off Miss Boot. Sooner or later she'd remember she was gasping for coffee and then what would happen? He imagined her drinking the potion and turning as green as a frog.

Know-All Nick set a test paper down on Bertie's desk.

"Feeling nervous, Bertie?" he smirked. "I do hope you've done your homework!"

"Course I have," lied Bertie.

Nick moved on to the next desk.

Dirty Bertie

"What on earth are you going to do?" hissed Eugene.

"About what?" asked Darren.

"The potion!" said Eugene.

"Eugene thinks it'll make Miss Boot sick," said Bertie. "What if her hair falls out?"

"HA HA!" laughed Darren. "It won't, will it?"

"How should I know?" moaned Bertie. "I've never made a magic potion before! It could do anything."

"SILENCE!" boomed Miss Boot. "There should be no need for talking. Right, you may all turn over your papers and begin."

Bertie read the first few questions. He hadn't the faintest idea what they meant. In any case, he had other things to worry about. He watched Miss Boot anxiously. Oh no, she was reaching for her flask again! She unscrewed the lid and placed the cup on her desk.

Bertie's hand shot up once more.

"What is it now?" groaned Miss Boot. "This better be important, Bertie."

"Um … can I get you a glass of water?" asked Bertie. "You must be thirsty doing all that talking."

"I've got my coffee, thank you," snapped Miss Boot.

"But water's better for you," argued Bertie.

"ENOUGH!" thundered Miss Boot. "Stop wasting time and get on with the test!"

Bertie gulped. He'd tried but it was hopeless. He watched in alarm as Miss

Dirty Bertie

Boot poured the murky brown liquid into her cup. Surely she'd notice that something wasn't right? But Miss Boot was too busy keeping an eye on her class. She raised the cup to her lips and took a large gulp. Bertie held his breath...

"BLEURGH!"

Dirty Bertie

Miss Boot spat the drink all over her desk. She stared down at her cup. Gloopy bits of something swam around on top.

"What on earth is this?" she spluttered.

Bertie gulped. At least Miss Boot hadn't turned green or sprouted horns. She rose to her feet. The class had all stopped writing.

"Whatever this is, it is *not* coffee," she said. "Somebody in this class has been playing tricks. At break time my flask went missing. One of you took it – WHO WAS IT?"

There was a terrible silence. Bertie slid down in his seat. *As long as no one talks, she can't prove anything*, he thought.

Dirty Bertie

Know-All Nick raised his hand.

"Please, miss, I think I know," he bleated. "At break I saw Bertie hiding something under his jumper. It looked like your flask."

Bertie closed his eyes. Trust blabbermouth Nick to ruin everything.

"BERTIE!" thundered Miss Boot. "Did you put something in my coffee?"

"Um … not exactly," squeaked Bertie.

"Then what, *exactly*?" demanded Miss Boot.

"I might have swapped your coffee for something else," admitted Bertie. "A sort of … um … magic potion."

Miss Boot's eyebrows shot up.

"A WHAT?"

"A magic potion," repeated Bertie. "It was nothing bad – just weeds, cobwebs and a bit of mud."

"MUD?" screeched Miss Boot. "You put mud in my coffee?"

"Just a little," said Bertie. "I only wanted you to forget the maths test."

"Ah, so now we're getting to the truth," said Miss Boot grimly. "Well, I hate to disappoint you, Bertie, but magic potions won't save you. You're going to

Dirty Bertie

take this test – not only today, but every day until you get full marks."

"*Full marks?*" groaned Bertie.

"That's right. And to help, here's a little light reading for homework," said Miss Boot, handing him an enormous book. "I'm sure it'll work like magic."

SLEEPOVER!

CHAPTER 1

Bertie's mum had taken him clothes shopping in town. They were just leaving Dibble's department store when Bertie stopped dead. A pale, smug-faced boy was heading their way with his mother. It was his sworn enemy, Know-All Nick.

Bertie tried to duck behind his mum but it was too late...

Dirty Bertie

"Hello, Bertie!" sang Nick.

"Hello, Nickerless," replied Bertie with a scowl.

"How lovely to bump into you!" trilled Nick's mum. "We haven't seen you since last parents' evening. And how is Bertie getting on at school?"

"Oh … yes, very well, thank you, Mrs Wormsley," said Mum.

This was news to Bertie. His last report was so bad he'd tried to lose it in the postbox.

"Of course, Nicholas is doing wonderfully well," Mrs Wormsley boasted. "We've just popped in to buy him a little treat for passing his piano exam, haven't we, poppet?"

Poppet? Bertie raised his eyebrows. Nick stuck out his tongue. The two

Dirty Bertie

mums carried on chatting and took out their phones to swap numbers.

"What's in the shopping bag?" asked Nick.

"None of your business," replied Bertie.

Nick snatched the bag.

"Ooh, new pants!" he jeered. "Spotty ones to match your face!"

Dirty Bertie

"Give them back!" cried Bertie.
"Anyway, what are you buying? Ugly
cream?"

"Actually, I'm getting a new ski
jacket," bragged Nick. "We're going
skiing after Christmas. I bet you've
never been."

"Course I have," snorted Bertie. At
least he'd been to the Snowdome,
which obviously counted. He tugged at
his mum's arm to go.

"Yes, all right, Bertie," said Mum.
"We'd better get on. Lovely to see
you."

"You too, and I'll be in touch," replied
Nick's mum.

"What was all that about?" asked
Bertie as they hurried away.

"Oh, she suggested you might like to

go for a sleepover some time," replied Mum.

A SLEEPOVER? Bertie almost walked into a lamppost.

"A sleepover – *with Nick?*" he wailed.

"Yes, it was kind of her, wasn't it?" said Mum.

"But it's Know-All Nick!" said Bertie. "I'm not going for a sleepover at his house!"

"Why not?" asked Mum.

"Because we're not even friends!" cried Bertie. "We're more like deadly enemies. Surely you know that?"

Dirty Bertie

"Well, I know he's not one of your best friends, but you are in the same class," said Mum.

"Loads of people are in my class but it doesn't make them my friends!" protested Bertie. "Nick's a know-all and a big head and he's always telling tales."

"I'm sure he isn't," said Mum. "Anyway, its only a sleepover. I could hardly say you wouldn't go."

".WHY NOT?" demanded Bertie.

Mum sighed. "Don't make such a fuss, Bertie. I expect his mum was just being polite. She'll probably forget she ever mentioned it."

Bertie certainly hoped so. A sleepover ... at Know-All Nick's house? He'd rather sleep in a cave with vampire bats!

CHAPTER 2

The following week Bertie was getting
ready for school. Downstairs he could
hear his mum talking on her phone.

"Yes, thank you, I'm sure Bertie will be
delighted."

He hurried down.

"Who was that?"

"That was Mrs Wormsley," said Mum.

"She's invited you for a sleepover with Nick this Friday."

Bertie's mouth fell open.

"You didn't say 'yes', did you?" he gulped.

"What else could I say?" asked Mum.

"Anything! Phone her back," begged Bertie. "Say I'm sick, say I've got toothache or brainache or something."

"I'm not telling lies," said Mum. "It's just for one night, it's not going to kill you."

"IT WILL!" moaned Bertie. "Anyway, I can't go on Friday because … Eugene's invited me for a sleepover at his house."

"You just made that up," said Mum. "Besides, it's all arranged now. You never know, you might actually enjoy it."

Enjoy it? thought Bertie, fat chance of that if Nick was going to be there.

Dirty Bertie

He slammed the front door and stomped off down the road. Wait until Darren and Eugene heard about this. At least they'd understand.

"A sleepover – with Know-All Nick?" giggled Darren. "HA HA! HEE HEE!"

Bertie folded his arms. His friends seemed to think it was the best joke they'd ever heard.

"It's not funny," he grumbled.

"It is pretty funny," said Darren.

"I wonder what you'll do all evening," said Eugene. "You could help Nick tidy his bedroom."

"Or do your homework together," said Darren.

Dirty Bertie

"It's too horrible for words," moaned
Bertie. "You've got to help me!"

"What can *we* do?" asked Eugene.
"I'm just amazed that Nick invited you."

"He didn't, that's the whole point!"
said Bertie. "It's all his mum's idea. He
probably hates it as much as I do…"

Bertie stopped dead. Wait a minute…

Dirty Bertie

Maybe it wasn't too late to get out of it?

"I'll be right back," Bertie told his friends. "I need to speak to Nick."

Know-All Nick was leaning against the railings, waiting for the bell to go.

"Hello, Nick!" said Bertie.

"Huh, it's you," said Nick, with an icy glare.

Bertie thought it was probably best to get straight to the point.

"Look, you know this sleepover on Friday!" he said. "I don't want to come."

"No kidding," sneered Nick. "Do you think it was my idea? I wouldn't invite you if you begged me on your knees."

"Well, I didn't," said Bertie. "It's bad enough seeing you at school every day, I don't want to see you at your house."

Dirty Bertie

"I can't think of anything worse!"
moaned Nick.

"For once we agree," said Bertie.
"Can't you get your mum to call it off?"

Nick shook his head. "I've tried," he
said. "I told her we're not friends. I said
you're smelly, you pick your nose and
you've got fleas – but she won't listen!
She says it's all arranged and it would be
rude to cancel."

"That's what my mum says too,"

sighed Bertie. "But there's got to be
something we can do."

"There isn't," said Nick. "Trust me, if
there was I'd have thought of it by now.
We're stuck with it."

Bertie gave up. It was all their mums'
fault, he thought bitterly. If they were so
keen on the idea, why didn't they have
their own sleepover?

CHAPTER 3

All too quickly, Friday arrived. Bertie usually looked forward to Fridays as the start of the weekend – no school, no Miss Boot and no one shouting at him to pay attention. Not this Friday though – he had a whole evening of Know-All Nick to endure.

At five o'clock Dad drove him over to

Dirty Bertie

Nick's house.

"Remember your manners," Dad said as he rang the doorbell. "And please *try* not to get into any trouble."

"When do I ever get in trouble?" asked Bertie.

Dad gave him a look – it would take too long to answer that question.

Mrs Wormsley opened the door. "Ah, Bertie, here you are!" she clucked. "Nicholas has been so looking forward to this, haven't you, bunnikins?"

Bunnikins looked like he wanted to crawl into a hole.

"Take Bertie's bag then, Nicholas, and show him where to leave his shoes," said Mrs Wormsley.

Nick's house was modern and shiny, like something in a magazine. Everything

Dirty Bertie

was spotlessly clean and smelled of
polish. Bertie had to leave his shoes by
the door. The lounge had a thick white
carpet. The sofas and chairs were white
leather. On every wall were photos
of Know-All Nick: Nick in his school
uniform, Nick on a sledge, Nick holding
a skinny cat that was trying to escape.

Dirty Bertie

"The carpet's brand new," said Mrs Wormsley proudly. "That's why we don't wear our shoes indoors. We don't want to get it dirty, do we?"

Bertie glanced at his grubby hands and stuffed them in his pockets. It was probably best not to touch anything.

"Well, why don't you boys run along and play while I get supper ready?" said Nick's mum.

Upstairs Nick's bedroom was nothing like Bertie's room. The floor wasn't covered in socks, toys and half-eaten biscuits. Nick's shirts, ties and jackets hung neatly on a rail. His prizes and certificates hung on the wall, along with every school report.

Nicholas is such a joy to teach! If only his classmates were more like him.

Dirty Bertie

Nick flopped down on his bed.

"So what do you want to do then?" he asked sulkily.

Bertie shrugged. "I dunno. What do you normally do on a sleepover?"

"I don't have many sleepovers," said Nick. "Other children are so boring. I could show you my coin collection, I suppose."

"No thanks," said Bertie.

"I know, why don't we play schools!" suggested Nick. "I'll be the teacher and set you lots of homework."

"You must be kidding," said Bertie. "Can't we go outside? I'll be a pirate captain and take you prisoner."

"No way," said Nick. "I don't like rough games."

Bertie rolled his eyes. If Darren and Eugene were here, they'd be building their own den and raiding the kitchen for a midnight feast. Nick had probably never had a midnight feast in his life!

"This is boring!" grumbled Nick. "I wish you'd just go home."

"Me too," said Bertie.

Nick lay back on his pillow, thinking. Suddenly he shot upright with an idea.

Dirty Bertie

"Listen, there's only one way you could go home – if my parents sent you," he said.

Bertie frowned. "Why would they do that?"

Nick smiled. "If you did something really, really bad."

"Oh, yeah, that's all right for you," said Bertie. "I'll be the one who gets in trouble."

Nick shrugged. "I'm never in trouble, I'm just no good at it," he said. "But you're always in trouble so it shouldn't be difficult. Anyway, don't you want to go home?"

Bertie considered it. It would mean joining forces with Nick, which was normally out of the question. But this was an emergency and it would put

an end to the world's worst sleepover.
He could be home eating pizza and
watching TV, while Nick could go back
to counting his coin collection.

"It's up to you," said Nick. "Or we
can just stay here and I'll show you my
certificates."

That settled it.

"Okay, I'm in," said Bertie. "What do
I have to do?"

CHAPTER 4

At six o'clock they sat down to supper.
Nick's mum had made watery vegetable
soup. Nick and his parents took dainty
sips from their spoons. Bertie glanced
at Nick who gave him a nod. Time for
"Operation Home Time". Bertie raised
his soup bowl to his lips.

"SHLUUUURPP!"

"Goodness!" cried Nick's mum. "Where are your manners, Bertie?"

"Sorry, that's how we eat soup at home," explained Bertie.

"Good heavens!" said Nick's dad. "Use your spoon, that's what it's for!"

Bertie picked up his spoon and shovelled soup into his mouth. Then he sat back, patted his stomach and gave a long, loud...

"BURRRRRRRRRP!"

It was one of his best, an absolute ripper. Nick's dad almost fell off his chair.

"REALLY!" he said. "I hope you don't do that at home?"

"Oh yes," replied Bertie. "Our family always has burping contests at the table. If you think I'm loud you should hear my mum!"

Dirty Bertie

Nick's mum and dad exchanged worried looks. The boy had no manners at all and his family sounded revolting.

Dessert was served. Bertie talked with his mouth full and wiped his nose on the tablecloth. He spilled trifle on his jumper and licked it off. Nick's mum tutted loudly while his dad looked like he might explode. Nevertheless Bertie was their guest and they pretended not to mind.

Dirty Bertie

After supper Bertie and Nick went back upstairs.

"It's not working," said Nick. "You need to try harder."

"I'm doing my best!" grumbled Bertie. "It's not easy being disgusting!"

He slumped on Nick's bed – it wasn't even seven o'clock. Unless he thought of something they had hours of boredom ahead. He looked out of the window. It had started to rain.

Bertie smiled. "You know I suggested playing pirates? How about we play outside?"

"Don't be stupid," said Nick. "We'd get soaking wet."

"Exactly. Wet *and* muddy," agreed Bertie. "And the thing about pirates is, they never take their boots off."

Dirty Bertie

Nick's eyes grew bigger. If Bertie meant what he thought, it would cause a riot.

"WE CAN'T!" he wailed. "My mum will go up the wall!"

"Probably," smiled Bertie. "You'll be sent to bed and I'll be sent home."

Dirty Bertie

Nick's parents were clearing up in the kitchen. Mr Wormsley closed the dishwasher.

"What's that horrible noise?" he asked.

They listened. Loud whoops and shrieks of excitement reached their ears. It sounded like it was coming from the garden.

"The boys are upstairs, aren't they?" asked Nick's mum.

She opened the back door and gasped. Bertie and her son were chasing each other round the garden. Their clothes were soaked and their shoes were caked in mud. A horrible thought crossed her mind. Stepping out, she saw that the French doors were wide open.

Dirty Bertie

Surely not?

She rushed back into the lounge.

"NOOOO!" she screamed. "MY BEAUTIFUL NEW CARPET!"

Dirty Bertie

A trail of footprints made a muddy pattern across the white carpet. Splodgy marks on the white sofa and chairs suggested pirates had been bouncing on them.

"NICHOLAS! BERTIE!" screeched Mrs Wormsley. "GET IN HERE RIGHT NOW!"

Things moved fairly quickly after that. Mr Wormsley phoned Bertie's parents to come and collect him. Nick was packed off to bed. As he went upstairs he glanced back at Bertie with a sly smile.

Bertie nodded to him.

During the drive home Bertie's dad kept a stony silence.

"Oh well," sighed Bertie. "I guess I won't be invited round for any more sleepovers."

Dirty Bertie

"No, I very much doubt it," said Dad through gritted teeth.

Bertie sat back and yawned happily. For a moment then, he'd almost enjoyed playing pirates in the rain. It wouldn't last, of course. On Monday, Nick would be back to his old smug self and the two of them would be at war again. Bertie couldn't wait.

BULLY!

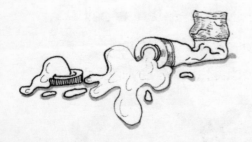

CHAPTER 1

Bertie and his friends were playing
cricket on the field before school.

TWHACK! Darren's bat cracked
the ball.

"Catch it, Bertie!" cried Eugene.

Bertie looked up as the tennis ball
rocketed towards him. At the last
minute he ducked. The ball bounced

once on the grass and ran away across the playground.

"Six!" cried Darren. "That's thirty-two not out."

Bertie pulled a face.

"Go on then, get it," said Darren.

Bertie trudged off. He couldn't see the point of cricket. Most of the time it involved fetching the ball so that Darren could wallop it somewhere else.

The ball had rolled to a stop at someone's feet. "Oh no," groaned Bertie. The feet belonged to Masher Martin, the biggest bully in the school!

Masher was in the top year. Next to Bertie and his friends, he looked like a giant – the kind that ate small children.

Masher bent down and picked up the ball.

"What's the problem?" asked Darren.

Bertie pointed.

"Oh no, not Masher Martin!" moaned Eugene.

"Just ask him to give the ball back," said Darren.

"YOU ask him," said Bertie.

"I'm batting, you're the fielder," argued Darren.

Bertie sighed.

"Why's it always left to me?" he muttered as he headed towards Masher.

Dirty Bertie

He'd heard all the stories. Masher had his own seat on the school bus and always pushed in to be first in the dinner queue. Once he'd dumped Trevor in a wheelie bin just for "staring at him". Even Mr Weakly was scared of Masher and he was a teacher!

"Hi, Masher," squeaked Bertie. "Actually, that's our ball."

Masher stared at him as if he was a small insect.

Bertie tried again.

"So anyway, could we have it back?"

Masher folded his arms. "Ask me nicely," he grunted.

Bertie glanced back at his friends. He knew this was a bad idea.

"Please, Masher, can we have our ball back?" he sighed.

Masher shrugged and held the tennis ball out to him. The moment Bertie reached for it, he snatched it away.

"HAR! HAR!" he hooted. "You know what? I think I'll keep it. Unless you want to argue?"

"ME?" said Bertie.

"Yeah YOU, maggot," growled Masher, leaning in close. Bertie did the only sensible thing – he turned and ran.

"Where's the ball?" asked Darren.

"He won't give it back," Bertie panted.

"But it's our ball, he can't just steal it!" cried Darren.

"Who's stealing?" whined a voice behind them.

Bertie swung round. Trust Know-All Nick to be earwigging on their conversation.

"Masher Martin's got our ball," explained Eugene. "Bertie asked but he won't give it back."

"Bertie? HA! HA!" jeered Nick. "I bet he was too scared to speak."

"I was not!" said Bertie. "Masher Martin doesn't scare me."

"Oh no?" said Nick.

"No," said Bertie. "He's just a big, ugly bully and one of these days I'll teach him a lesson."

Dirty Bertie

The words were out before he could stop them. Nick looked delighted.

"Well, I'm sure Masher would be very interested to hear that!" he smirked.

Bertie stared. "No, wait … you're not actually going to tell him?"

"Why not?" said Nick. "You wanted to teach him a lesson, well this could be your big chance!"

He patted Bertie on the back and walked off, wearing a huge grin.

"Uh-oh. Now you've done it!" said Darren.

"What did you say that for?" asked Eugene.

"He's bluffing," said Bertie. "He wouldn't really tell Masher, would he?"

"I wouldn't put it past him," said Eugene. "And then you're *really* in big trouble."

CHAPTER 2

All that morning Bertie found it impossible to concentrate. Miss Boot droned on about commas and full stops but he didn't hear a word. He kept expecting to see Masher's big, ugly face at the door. He couldn't remember exactly what he'd said but the words "teach him a lesson" stuck in his mind.

Dirty Bertie

What on earth made him say it?
Couldn't he keep his big mouth shut for
once? If Masher ever found out, he was
toast. His only chance was to lie low and
keep out of sight.

At break time, Bertie hid behind
Darren and Eugene.

"What are you playing at?" asked
Darren.

"I don't want to run into Masher," said
Bertie. "Can you see him?"

Darren looked around the playground.

"He's over there talking to someone,"
he said.

"Not just someone, it's Know-All
Nick," said Eugene.

"You're kidding!" groaned Bertie.
"What are they saying?"

"How should we know?" said Darren.

Dirty Bertie

"Watch out, they're coming over!"

Bertie panicked. He had to hide and quickly! He dived behind a bench and lay flat on his belly, his heart pounding. Darren and Eugene sat down to try and hide him. Seconds later, footsteps approached.

"Where's Bertie?" whined Nick.

"Yeah, where's the maggot?" grunted Masher.

"We haven't seen him," lied Darren.

"No, I think he probably went home," said Eugene.

Nick narrowed his eyes.

"Liars!" he said.

Getting down on all fours, he peered under the bench.

"Oh, there you are, Bertie!" he crowed. "Hiding away like a little mouse!"

Bertie crawled out. "I was ... just looking for my hanky," he explained.

Nick pointed.

"That's him," he said. "He's the one I told you about."

"I didn't!" said Bertie.

"Didn't what?" growled Masher.

Dirty Bertie

"I didn't call you 'a big, ugly bully'," said Bertie.

"Told you," said Nick. "And that's not all. He's going to teach you a lesson, isn't that right, Bertie?"

"NO!" wailed Bertie. "I was talking about someone else!"

Masher grabbed him by his shirt, lifting him clean off the ground.

"You and me, on the field after school," he said. "Got it, maggot?"

"Yes, got it!" croaked Bertie.

Masher set him down.

"Be there or I'll come looking," he snarled. "Don't forget!"

Dirty Bertie

He stomped away, clearing a wide path through the other children.

"What's he mean: 'Me and him on the field'? Are we playing cricket?" asked Bertie.

"Don't be stupid," sneered Nick. "He's going to fight you."

"FIGHT ME?" gasped Bertie, his voice rising in panic.

A fight with Masher Martin, the biggest bully in the school? He was going to need a suit of armour.

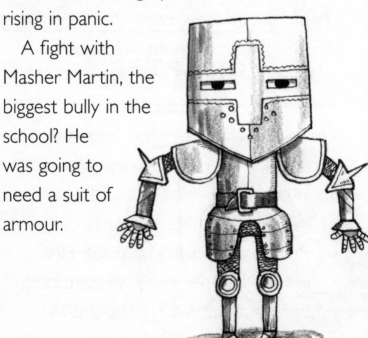

CHAPTER 3

After break, they had Art. Bertie
perched on a stool while Darren and
Eugene painted splodgy portraits of him.

"Keep still. Don't talk and don't
fidget," boomed Miss Boot.

But Bertie couldn't keep still. He
jiggled his legs nervously. All he could
think about was facing Masher after

school. He'd never fought anyone in
his life. What was the point of fighting
anyway? Someone always got hurt and
in this case it would be him!

"Sit still!" grumbled Darren.

"I CAN'T!" moaned Bertie. "Listen,
why don't we all fight him? With three
of us we'd stand a chance."

"No fear, he's massive!" said Eugene.
"Anyway, my mum doesn't like me
fighting."

"Size isn't everything," said Darren.
"You could try judo on him."

"I don't know any judo," moaned
Bertie.

"Neither do I," said Darren. "But I've
seen it on the telly."

"You know what you should do? Tell a
teacher," said Eugene. "Tell Miss Boot."

Dirty Bertie

"You think she'd listen?" asked Bertie.

"BERTIE! What did I just say?" barked Miss Boot. "Stop talking!"

Bertie decided he was in enough trouble already. What if Masher found out he'd gone running to a teacher? If only he could leave school before the bell went! Actually, that wasn't a bad idea...

His eyes fell on the tube of red paint Darren was using. That might do the trick. When no one was looking, he squeezed a blob on to his finger and hid the tube in his pocket. Now to get Miss Boot's attention.

"ARGHH! OWW!" he howled.

"What's the matter, Bertie?" groaned Miss Boot.

"I've cut my finger! It's bleeding!" cried Bertie.

Dirty Bertie

Miss Boot marched over. She seized Bertie's finger to examine it.

"Do I need to go to hospital?" asked Bertie hopefully.

"I doubt it, that's red paint," snapped Miss Boot. "Do you think I was born yesterday?"

"Nice try, Bertie," grinned Darren.

Bertie shook his head. There was no escape. At home time Masher Martin would be waiting for him on the field. At least the fight would be over quickly. He'd probably pass out before they started.

CHAPTER 4

Bertie watched the clock hands creep closer to home time. Maybe Masher Martin wouldn't turn up? Maybe he'd done enough bullying for one day? The bell rang and Bertie jumped out of his skin.

He trailed out of school with Darren and Eugene. A small crowd had

Dirty Bertie

gathered on the field. Know-All Nick was there – obviously he'd spread the word about the fight of the century: Masher Martin v Wimpy Bertie.

"OH, BERTIE! Over here!" sang Nick. "We're all waiting for you!"

Bertie's heart sank.

"It's no good," said Darren. "You'll just have to stand up to him."

"It's not too late," said Eugene. "I could still find a teacher."

Bertie wished he'd listened earlier. Right now he would have been relieved to see Miss Boot or even Mr Weakly. Where were all the teachers when you needed one?

Dirty Bertie

It was too late now because Masher Martin had arrived.

"Right then, maggot," he growled. "Let's get started."

Bertie felt his legs turn to jelly.

"Remember, keep moving," Darren whispered. "Tire him out then hit him with the judo moves I showed you."

The crowd had formed a rough circle with Bertie in the middle. He looked round. Darren gave him a thumbs up but Eugene had vanished. *So much for friends!* thought Bertie.

"What's the matter? Not trying to chicken out, Bertie?" jeered Nick.

Masher lumbered forward. Bertie took Darren's advice and danced out of reach. They circled round to the left, then back to the right.

Dirty Bertie

"Keep still!" growled Masher. "You're making me dizzy."

Suddenly he made a grab for Bertie. Bertie dodged out of reach and crawled through his legs. Masher whirled round, but Bertie wasn't there. He'd jumped on Masher's back and was clinging on for dear life.

"GET OFF ME!" roared Masher.

Dirty Bertie

He twisted this way and that, trying to shake Bertie loose. But Bertie hung on tight, knowing he was safer where he was. The crowd started cheering. No one liked the school bully so they were all supporting Bertie.

"Hang on, Bertie! You're on top!" shouted Darren.

This was sort of true but not for long. The next moment Masher swung round and Bertie lost his grip. He was thrown off, landing on the grass with a thump. Something in his pocket squelched. Bertie looked up and saw Masher's big, ugly face grinning down at him. So this was it – curtains – he was a goner.

Suddenly Masher gaped, his eyes wide with panic.

"W-what's that?" he gasped, pointing.

"It's not blood?"

Bertie looked down at his jeans.
A large red patch had spread from his
pocket. It certainly looked like blood…

"ARGHH! URGHH!" moaned Bertie,
clutching his side.

"Now you've done it," said Darren.
"Better call an amblance."

Masher had turned very pale.

"But … I didn't touch him! It wasn't
my fault!" he wailed.

"Try telling that to Miss Boot," said
Darren. "Here she comes!"

Bertie sneaked a look. Miss Boot was
striding furiously towards them with
Eugene at her side. Masher didn't wait
to explain. He fled across the field with
a wail of terror.

"HEEEEELP!"

"What's going on?" thundered Miss Boot. "I will NOT have fighting in school!"

"I wasn't fighting!" said Bertie. "He was fighting me!"

"Telltale!" muttered Nick.

"QUIET, Nicholas!" snapped Miss Boot. "I'm surprised at you. From what I hear you're the one who started all this."

Nick turned crimson.

"Well, Bertie, are you actually hurt?" asked Miss Boot, holding out a hand.

Bertie got to his feet.

"Not really. I'm feeling much better now," he said.

Miss Boot folded her arms. "Next time someone tries to bully you, come and tell me right away," she said. "Do you understand?"

Bertie nodded.

"I will deal with Mr Martin in the morning. And you too, Nicholas," said Miss Boot. She glanced at Bertie's red stained jeans. "As for you, Bertie, if that's what I think it is, you better get those jeans in the wash."

"Yes, Miss Boot," mumbled Bertie. "And, um, thanks."

Dirty Bertie

They headed out of the gate and turned for home. Bertie could hardly believe his luck. For once Miss Boot hadn't shouted at him … in fact she'd actually taken his side! He doubted if Masher Martin or Nick would get off so lightly tomorrow morning. He noticed Eugene staring at him.

"That stuff on your jeans – it's not blood at all, is it?" said Eugene.

"Of course not!" laughed Darren.

Bertie put his hand in his pocket and produced a messy tube of red paint.

"I forgot this was in my pocket," he said. "I guess it must have burst open when I landed on the grass."

Eugene grinned. "Trust you, Bertie!"

"Well, it certainly fooled Masher," said Darren. "You should have seen his face when I said Miss Boot was coming!"

"Serves him right for being such a big bully," said Bertie. "I told you."

"Told us what?" asked Eugene.

"I told you I'd teach him a lesson one day!"